James Marriott

Political Considerations

being a few thoughts of a candid man at the present crisis, in a letter to a

noble lord retired from power

James Marriott

Political Considerations
being a few thoughts of a candid man at the present crisis, in a letter to a noble lord retired from power

ISBN/EAN: 9783337381011

Printed in Europe, USA, Canada, Australia, Japan

Cover: Foto ©Andreas Hilbeck / pixelio.de

More available books at **www.hansebooks.com**

POLITICAL

CONSIDERATIONS

At the PRESENT CRISIS.

[Price Eighteen-pence.]

Political Confiderations;

BEING A
FEW THOUGHTS
OF A
CANDID MAN
AT THE
PRESENT CRISIS.

In a Letter to a Noble Lord retired from Power.

CONCORDIAE

LONDON,
Printed for J. HINXMAN, at the Globe in Pater-
nofter Row. 1762.

——————Magno in populo cum sæpe coorta eſt
Seditio, ſævitque animis ignobile vulgus,
Jamque faces et ſaxa volant, furor arma miniſtrat,
Tum pietate gravem, ac meritis, ſi forte virum quem
Conſpexere, ſilent, arrectis auribus aſtant;
Ille regit dictis animos, et pectora mulcet.

VIRGIL.

A

FEW THOUGHTS

OF A

CANDID MAN

AT THE

PRESENT CRISIS.

In a LETTER to a NOBLE LORD.

My Lord,

YOU, who are allowed by your enemies and friends to have as much
good-nature as any man living, will,
I hope, readily pardon the freedom and length
of this addrefs. I know there are people
who think you have paid more attention to
gaining the former than to retaining the latter,

B   how-

however tried and inviolably attached to you;
whether this exceeding fociality of your humour, or political opinion of your fuppofed
interefts, deferves the blame of your friends,
I will not venture to fay; but from one of
your friends you are at liberty to fuppofe
that the prefent addrefs is offered to your
perufal, at a time when you have leifure
both to read and think. It matters very
little to your Grace, who it is fets you upon
thinking. No doubt, if you are pleafed to
think at all, you will think rightly, after
having acquired fuch deep experience of men
and things, in the courfe of near half a
century, in the heat of public affairs.

My Lord, the happinefs you may now
enjoy in your retreat from power is a fubject,
I humbly fubmit it to you, not unworthy
your moft ferious contemplation. The reflections arifing from it may have an influence
very ufeful upon your conduct for the reft of
your days, if it is at all important to you to
con-

continue the poffeffing your mind in that tranquillity which muft be wifhed for by every good and wife man, and which fhould precede and attend the clofing of that great part you have fo long played with activity and with honour.

But, my Lord, although it is eafy to know when we have done well, it is a very hard thing to know when we have done enough. *Manum tollere de tabulâ* was a leffon which a great artift among the antients complained he could never teach to one of his moft celebrated fcholars. A warmth of imagination, a certain reftlefsnefs of difpofition, or, in other words, a love to be doing, occafioned him often to fpoil the beft picture, I mean beft when left at a certain point of perfection, becaufe he could not help returning frequently to the piece, and again working over and confufing the fame colours by a handling too bufy.

How

How often has the fame difpofition been
feen in many great men, who have never
left public affairs till affairs have left them?
Had they fortunately known the juft point
where to have ftopped, they would have been
happy, adored, and perhaps immortalized.

But, my Lord, this inclination to be bufy
without end, is not yours, I believe; for I
believe willingly what I hope reafonably.
You are happy, very happy, in your retirement, in your reflections upon what is paft
or is to come, in being approved by your
Sovereign and the people, unpenfioned, un-
prejudiced, and mafter of yourfelf. Your
ftudies, your amufements, your duties of life,
are all your own, and, although in a private
ftation, you are not forgot to have fpent
your life and fortune in the fervice of your
Prince and country, and for the once doubt-
ful eftablifhment of a family now feated
firmly on the throne of thefe kingdoms.

Give

Give me leave to expatiate a little more with you, on the fubject of your retirement from power. You have been long a Minifter, be once, for once, the Philofopher.

It has been faid, that no man can be accounted happy till the end of his life, and it may be faid, with equal propriety, that no man can be accounted truly great till the end of his power. The firft was the anfwer of no lefs a perfon than the legiflator of the Athenian commonwealth to the queftion of a monarch, and the latter obfervation, I believe you will allow it, may find an example in a ftate as free and as polifhed, I may add too, as changeable as Athens. The hiftory of that celebrated republic very early has inftructed us, that every perfon, who undertakes the adminiftration of public affairs among a free people, muft expect fooner or later a reverie of his authority. Fatal indeed was the reverfe in that nation, which erected ftatues, not till after death, to the memory of its great
men,

men, after having firft banifhed them, or deprived them of life, upon fome fudden change of popular opinion.

Without mentioning the military leaders among the Athenians, who fuffered from this uncertainty of the popular humour, it is fufficient to mention Ariftides and Phocion, both of them remarkable for the integrity of their conduct in civil affairs, and their contempt of wealth ; both fharers in one common fate, that of their virtues not being fully known till they had ceafed to exert them for the public fervice.

How void of pain muft fuch a removal from power be, when attended with the confcioufnefs of having acted with integrity ? but how glorious, if that confcioufnefs is feconded, not by the tardy gratitude of pofterity, but by the prefent voice of the public? We cannot doubt but that a plaudite, beftowed in fuch a manner, is well deferved

by

by him who quits the ftage with fo peculiar
a grace; and when the leader of a ftate is
thus honourably levelled with his fellow-
citizens, we may juftly congratulate him upon the opportunity of adorning the remainder
of his life with the calm and virtuous dignity of a private ftation.

The direction of a capricious, ever difcontented, and jealous people, is always an
ungrateful, and often a dangerous tafk, in
the relinquifhing of which it is perhaps well
worth the retiring, were it only to look back,
in the hour of tumult, upon thofe feas from
which few other great men have efcaped with
honour, if with life, and to fee the ftorm
roll over in fecurity. If the knowledge of
truth is any defirable acquifition, this too is
the acquifition of a retreat from power.
A leifure for reflection, for liberal amufements,
and the ingenuous converfation of men of
merit, is fomething valuable to perfons capable
of tafting its pleafures and fhining in it, and
will

will always make fufficient amends for the defertion of fuch attendants as thofe are who are only fuffered to be familiar with greatnefs, becaufe they have juft genius enough to contrive the being fometimes neceffary to its fupport.

My Lord, it is my great concern, from the zeal I have for your real interefts and honour, that men of this caft, in the prefent difficult and important crifis, may poffibly attempt urging you to quit your private ftation, and to embark once more, upon their account only, in a bufy, factious, and turbulent world fo late in life. Your firft fcheme and declarations to all your friends did honour to your wifdom and moderation, that you would retire without a penfion, though not rich, and without anger, though you thought yourfelf a little neglected. I am fure many a true friend of your Grace has often applauded that refolution, however greatly his own interefts in your good-will to him may fuffer now by

your

your continuance in the fame difpofitions. Such a friend, if you confulted him, would affure you, that he dreads really nothing fo much, for your own fake, as to fee you attempting to run again the race of public life with a new generation of young men, who have fprung up, the children of your cotemporaries, in a new field of action, of new notions, and a quite altered world. To do fo would be to facrifice your repofe, and probably the reputation you now fo highly poffefs with your country and the world.

On the other hand, difappointed men, accuftomed to venality, and expecting nothing from a fyftem of government that begins with views of reforming abufe in offices, of a free, uncorrupt parliament, and under a Prince not addicted to the pleafures of a vicious life, will naturally wifh to fee things put again upon the old footing, I mean that when government was under peculiar neceffities; and they will therefore act upon the fame

C   prin-

principles and confiderations as thofe which induced the noble youth of Rome to attempt to overthrow the eftablifhment of a virtuous republic in its infancy. They obferved, that, under the former eftablifhment, *effe a quo impetres, ubi jus, ubi injuria opus fit, effe gratiæ locum, effe beneficio, et irafci et ignofcere poffe: inter amicum et inimicum difcrimen noffe*; but that the fcheme of adminiftration now founded upon principles ill fuited to corrupt men, accuftomed to all the advantages of party, and to the long poffeffion of royal favour, was *rem furdam, inexorabilem; falubriorem melioremque inopi quam potenti, nihil laxamenti nec veniæ habere; fi modum excefferis periculofam effe; in tot humanis erroribus folam innocentiam vivere.* How eafy then is it, my Lord, for fuch a fort of men as I have defcribed to form an oppofition, to raife a clamour, and to increafe their party againft the meafures of any Sovereign in a free country, determined to reign and to be obeyed only upon principles of integrity, moderation, and virtue?

But

But I cannot conceive that you, my Lord, can ever be perfuaded by fuch men as thefe are to join with any fuch oppofition, and to fet up a ftandard for their adherents to refort to, in order to combat dangers to the conftitution, which are feen only to exift through the medium of their particular paffions and interefts, and to oppofe even the authority of the throne itfelf. I think that, of all men, you, my Lord, will be the laft to abet factions and republican principles in the ftate. You have ever publicly held, that oppofition to the fervants of the King and people, in times of difficulty and danger, is an oppofition to the conftitution itfelf: that, in fuch a cafe, the general interefts of the nation are fure to fuffer, and that therefore no crime is greater than that of a fet of men, ftopping by violence the great machine of government, till fuch time as their vanity, ambition, or avarice fhall be gratified at the public expence, and even entailed upon pofterity.

No

No body is better acquainted than yourfelf, my Lord, with how much unhappy
fcandal to government men of faces and fpi-
rits not eafily afhamed or daunted have re-
ceived the wages of calumny and vociferation.
The very remedies applied, with the beft
intentions, to faction at different times, have
increafed the evil of it; and to fuch un-
juftifiable oppofitions may be attributed many
weaknefles of the ftate, many indecifive fteps
in the fervants of the crown and people; for,
while the interefts and the contrivances of
factious and able men frequently difconcerted
the beft intentioned fchemes of adminiftration,
nothing was to be hoped for or expected from
the wifdom and integrity or even courage of
the beft minifter thus encumbered and embarraffed.

Too often, in refpect to this country, may
be applied the reflection of the Roman hifto-
rian:

Dum

Dum ad se quisque omnia trahit, nihil reli-
quum esse virium in medio, distractam lacera-
tamque rempublicam magis quorum in manu sit,
quam ut incolumis sit quæri.

I believe, my Lord, you will acknowledge
the picture I have drawn to be a true one.
You have found men to be the same in every
period of your life. You are no stranger to
the undertaking of the great task, never to
be accomplished, of obliging every one. You
know that nothing can satisfy discontented
tempers, nothing oblige ungrateful ones. You
are very sensible, that there is no difficulty in
making an opposition popular, and rendering
the many dupes to the interests of a few.
Such, my Lord, is the malignity of human
nature, in the general view of it, that almost
every man, excepting some few persons of
your Grace's generosity of disposition, hears
the accusation of a superior with pleasure; as
if the degradation of a higher character was
a real elevation of his own: besides that it is a

much

much eafier bufinefs to oppofe than to defend. The vivacity of the attack furprizes the auditor, the vehemence of it engages his attention, and the courage of it conciliates his favour. It is the delight of every ordinary mind to judge others, to criticife minutely, to new model every thing by its own ideas, to raife and to pull down. To this obvious caufe it muft be attributed, that, in all ages and in all free governments, every orator who watches the temper of the people, is fure to be heard with applaufe, and to draw after him, like the figure of the Gaulifh Hercules in the antique, his multitude by the ears.

There are feldom wanting opportunities for the exertion of fuch powers in a free country. Medical Authors obferve that every year has its peculiar and predominant difeafe; and it feems that in the fame manner every free country has, at certain periods, its peculiar political mania. The more popular every conftitution of government becomes, the

the more liable it is to the violence of thefe phrenfies. Our countrymen, my Lord, generally of an atrabilaire and aduft temperament, are very apt to be feized with them: in fuch a ftate of difcompofure they are eafily inflamed to a very unhappy excefs, and when once they lay afide that good fenfe and good humour for which they are remarkable above all other nations in Europe, the dreadful extremities to which they have paffed have been marked with blood in the annals of our hiftory. You, my Lord, remember times when the crown fhook on the head of the Sovereign; when the laws were almoft filent in the midft of arms; when a mob was oppofed to a mob, and the leaders of the ftate became of neceffity the conductors of a rabble.

It will be no wonder then if prefent or approaching times fhould afford us the fame miferable fpectacle of faction fo much to be lamented. The colours may indeed be different,

ent, but the effects of human paffions will be
for ever the fame.

The prefent crifis of this country, my
Lord, with regard to its affairs both at home
and abroad, is the moft difficult and important one fince we have been a people: and
the permanency of every blefling we enjoy
under Providence depends upon our unanimity, from the diffolution of which only can
our enemies form any hopes of overturning
the column of national glory and happinefs
fo lately and fo highly raifed, at the expence
of fo much blood and treafure poured forth
with prodigality. That a nation divided
againft itfelf cannot ftand, however brilliant
its victories, however powerful its alliances
and its refources may be, and however extenfive its expectations, is a truth that wants
no facred authority to prove it; and the
hiftory of all ages prefents to our minds the
terrible image of the once nobleft fpectacle
under heaven, of great, wife, and free nations
deprived

deprived of power, knowledge, liberty, and
funk into flavery, ignorance, weaknefs, and
barbarity; the effect of faction.

You therefore, my Lord, at this important crifis, in diffenting, as I make no doubt
you will diffent, from every unreafonable
fcheme of factious oppofition to government,
and in refufing to lend the affiftance of your
friends to the private views of any particular
fet of men, if any fuch fcheme is really
formed, will fhew, not only the important
weight you retain in the fcale of government,
by the effect which your neutrality, and dif-
approbation of violent means, will produce,
but you will act in a private ftation a public
part, the moft replete with glory to your own
character, confiftent with your general conduct towards your country and your Sovereign, and which will pafs your name down
to pofterity as a true and faithful fervant of
the crown with a more illuftrious title than
the Greateft Monarchs can beftow, in the

D   utmoft

utmoft plenitude of their power, the title of an Honeft man, without prejudice and without refentment.

The Heroes of antiquity, who are faid to have combated monfters, and were therefore deified, were, when divefted of the covering of mythology, no other perfons than men devoted to the good of the country in which they lived, which they adorned with laws, with arts, and arms, who quelled tyrants of every kind and deftroyed the power of faction and prejudice, and refifted the madnefs of the people as well as that of their leaders.

I imagine, my Lord, you will leave now the active parts of this Heroic patriotifm to younger men than yourfelf, who poffefs the fame parts and vivacity which diftinguifhed you fo early in life. Much may be expected from them when warmed by your example, and formed by your admonitions and expe- rience. I imagine that in the mean time you

you will content yourfelf with reftraining, by
your influence, the more vehement part of
your friends from diftreffing his Majefty and
the public, and with encouraging others, in-
timidated or mifled, to give all poffible aid
and affiftance to government.

His Majefty, at the beginning of his reign,
was pleafed to declare his defire of the affiftance of every good and honeft man in carrying on the great bufinefs of his government.
And if ever there was a period, through all
the annals of the Britifh hiftory, in which that
affiftance was peculiarly neceffary to the Sovereign and the true interefts of his people, it is
fo in the higheft degree at the prefent crifis;
the exceffive difficulty and importance of
which make it the duty of every good and
honeft man, as a member of the community,
to fupport, fo far as his influence may extend,
the meafures of his Majefty, independently
of any men who now are, or who have been
till now his fervants, and of all other perfonal
confiderations.   D 2   Un-

Unhappily for their Sovereign and their country, often many of the beft and ableft men, whofe influence and concurrence in the public fervice would be of the utmoft utility, are thofe who ftand leaft forward to promote it, who, either unwilling to draw with others in a fubordinate part, from too great a con-fcioufnefs of their own abilities, or who, content to purfue their own private affairs, amufements, or duties in the latent paths of life, leave the hard tafk of directing the public opinion, of combating prejudices, whe-ther old or new, equally deftructive of the common intereft, of refifting the violence of factious and corrupted men, of finding out frefh refources for every exigence of govern-ment, of fupplying the nerves of an extenfive war, or laying the foundations of a folid and lafting peace, who leave, I fay, thefe very arduous tafks to one almoft alone in the public fervice, obedient to the commands of his Sovereign and his duty, the object of private envy, and all the virulence of public faction.

Such

Such men like Atticus may fuffer the ftate to perifh, rather than hazard their own tranquillity or reputation in imitating a Cicero or a Cato, by flinging their weight into the ballance at a time when the affiftance of all might preponderate to the prefervation of all.

But you, my Lord, who never felt an indifference to the fate of your country, will not think that fuch a neglect of its interefts can be juftified eafily in any man, fince there is no man fcarcely fo contemptible in his abilities or connections, but he may add his mite in fome way or other to the general ftock, and do fome fervice to his country. Whoever the man is who thinks that the difcharge of private duties will excufe a total neglect of all public ones, he is certainly miftaken in point of morals, and is fo too in point of his own intereft, if it is true, that whatever paffes in government neceffarily comes home in its effects to the peace and property of every private man,

man, according to the plain maxim of the good old Roman, *publica prodendo tua nequic-quam ferves.*

But what fhall we fay, my Lord, if there are any men, I hope there are not any fuch men, who not only refufe to ferve in concurrence with another fervant of their prince, but who are determined to oppofe and embarrafs the counfels of their Sovereign, becaufe they are not allowed to have the fole direction and execution of them ? I am bold to declare, that if under fuch prefling difficulties a peace becoming neceffary fhould be made inadequate to the fanguine expectations of a people blooded with conqueft, and perhaps immoderate in fome of its expectations, the imperfections of that peace muft be imputed moft juftly to the men who fhall refufe their affiftance to make the peace or carry on the war.

Whenever therefore that event of peace fhall happen, let it be afked any candid man, whe-

whether in common juftice thofe perfons only ought to be poffeffed of the popular approbation and applaufe, who, when the veffel is
in a ftorm, weakened by a long and dangerous voyage, and now driving among rocks
and quickfands, quit the veffel with precipita-
tion, and without fuffering their friends to
touch one rope or oar, leave the helm to a
fingle perfon, faithful indeed to his duty, but
unequal perhaps in ftrength without fome affiftance to carry the veffel fafe into harbour,
leave it too determined to perfecute and purfue the fervant of the public for any ill confequences of their own conduct with all that
vengeance with which the never-forgiving
and unjuft temper of mankind conftantly purfues thofe it has injured moft.

Such an unfortunate fituation of this country, my Lord, is not, I truft, now exifting,
and it is to be hoped never will exift; but
that it may not be the cafe, every effort of
good and honeft men ought to be exerted to
pre-

prevent it, and to fupport at this crifis the meafures of his Majefty in the perfon of his fervants. The voice, the genius, the influence of
all able and difinterefted men fhould unite to
preferve that important concord of all orders
in the ftate, which till this threatening and
dark period has remained long unbroken, and
has made this little ifland to become the center of univerfal commerce, and maritime dominion, a great and mighty nation, which is
the aftonifhment of the prefent, and will be
the wonder of future ages.

My Lord, in order to form a juft idea of
a right plan of conduct for men of calm, candid, and difinterefted difpofitions to purfue at
this juncture, who, have any weight in government, we fhould do well, I humbly apprehend, to take a general view of the circumftances, under which his Majefty, his immediate fervants, and the interefts of this nation
both at home and abroad are underftood to
be at this particular period.

It

It is with the utmost concern and indignation that every good subject must have seen the base and daring attempts of men of very low reputation and abilities to render contemptible and unpopular the character of their Sovereign, and who have taken the advantage of a time for insulting Majesty itself with impunity, when the accumulated difficulties of government crowd upon the throne. What a situation is this for a young prince who discovers how much his inexperience of public life, of the manners and passions of unreasonble and corrupt men is unequal to his own intentions and integrity, and to the dictates of a heart overflowing with goodness to his own subjects and all mankind! Embarrassed by the evils of an enormous and extensive war begun before his reign, and in a long series of events encreasing with the load of government at the same time all the feebleness of it, he must with the deepest concern find himself not only encumbered with the management of precarious alliances, with the stubborn oppositi-

on

on of foreign and inveterate enemies, render-
ed defperate by their loffes, and with the
jealoufy and envy of neighbouring and powerful ftates, but above all muft he feel feverely
the neceffity of refifting any faction at home.
I do not fay, my Lord, that fuch a faction
exifts; I hope it does not againft the crown:
but I am at liberty to fuppofe, nay more, to
expect it: From the nature of man virtues always will meet refiftance in this world from
their oppofite vices. From the moment his
Majefty afcended the throne with the applaufe
of all men, it was eafy to forefee that the
glory which his uncommon virtues fpread
over his diadem, muft have its fhades. Is it
poffible to attempt deftroying the doctrine of
infernal dæmons, that men being corrupt and
wicked in general, cannot be governed but
upon corrupt and wicked principles, and not
to expect a fevere oppofition to even the beft
of Sovereigns? In fuch a cafe the youth of a
Sovereign will naturally be fet light of by men
hackneyed in the ways of the world, and
grown

grown ftubborn in iniquity : his firmnefs and
magnanimity will be reprefented as obftina-
cy, his frugality as fordidnefs; if he employs
his hours indefatigably in the high and labo-
rious duties of his exalted ftation, if he neither breaks in upon the peace or property
of any of his fubjects for vicious gratificati-
ons of pleafure, or the dangerous views of ambition, but filently purfues one fteady path
of uncommon virtue, ardent to become a
blefling to his own fubjects, and to be the
delight of mankind, that very conduct will
produce the moft malignant envy, even at the
foot of the throne.

I am forry to have occafion to obferve,
that princes, and even private men, have often more authority from their vices than from
their virtues over the minds of others; bad
men whenever they oppofe themfelves to good
ones, will never want adherents, they need
but ftamp with their feet, and there will
arife legions to fupport their caufe. What

re-

refources are there to be found in the paffions of mankind! avarice, luxury, profufion and indigence, long habituated to feed from the hand of corruption will all rife in arms, and promife very probable hopes of placing at the moft exalted point of power any one who will undertake to be the great difpenfer of corruption. Whenever he fhall wave his golden wand, the dæmons of vice will furround his circle.

Yet, my Lord, I believe you will agree with me in thinking, that if it is poffible to put the reins of government at any time into the hands of virtue, it is poffible to do it with the greateft hopes of fuccefs at the beginning of a reign, when the prince declares himfelf the enemy of corruption, and requires nothing of his people but to be free; when the reafons pleaded for encouraging venality no longer fubfift in the firm eftablifhment of the throne, once in danger from a foreign pretender, but now filled by a Sovereign born

in

in this country, and at a time too when the fate of the nation, in the greateſt criſis of its affairs, depends upon the virtue of every order of men amongſt us.

How happy an opportunity is there then offered, under theſe circumſtances, of deſtroying, or rather ſuffering to die away, all antient diſtinctions ſo fatal to the common good, which would certainly periſh of themſelves, ſince the object of them is no more, if they are not kept alive by the induſtry of factious and deſigning men for their own private purpoſes of ambition? You, my Lord, have been combating diſtinctions all your life, while they exiſted in reality and acquired due influence from thoſe combats in the mind of your Sovereign; and it muſt make a peculiar part of the happineſs of your life, that it has been extended to a period when you might ſee and congratulate the fortune of your country upon a ſituation of it when theſe miſerable and odious diſtinctions may ſafely, ly, and therefore ought to be totally annihilated.

My Lord, let us confider the fituation of the immediate fervant of the Crown, and the difficulties which attend him at this crifis, and confequently the reafonablenefs and juftice of not increafing thofe difficulties by a parliamentary or popular oppofition to the meafures which it may become the duty of his office to carry into execution.

In difcuffing every queftion of importance relating to the public interefts too much candour cannot be exerted, nor too much moderation confulted, in feparating the grounds of popular difcontent. It is highly ufeful to diftinguifh the Sovereign from his fervant, and the people from the dependents of a particular faction, and to enquire whether an oppofition is formed againft the man, or directed againft the meafures ? It is very unhappy both for the Prince and people that the

the latter are accuftomed to make few fuch neceffary diftinctions, but to look upon the immediate fervant of the Crown as the only perfon among the general fervants of the King and people to whom they are to place the whole account of the good and evil of government. Men therefore factioufly difpofed, and interefted in a change of the adminiftration, have little elfe to do, in order to effect it, but to render the immediate agent of the Sovereign ridiculous and unpopular by falfe accufations and reports, or by invidious diftinctions. To what a fhameful degree of indecency fuch kind of attempts have been often carried, I need not mention. Our conftitution indeed feems to favour fome licentioufnefs of this fort. It is true that all attacks within doors and without upon the Minifter, as he is called, do not affect the fafety of the Sovereign, but they prevent the Sovereign from doing all the good he intends, and deprive him of every means of carrying on the ordinary bufinefs of his government, without he will lean on a party for it; which, whenever it is the cafe, is fure to feize every poft in the ftate, to ftand between the King and the people till both are fubdued by the power of an oligarchy, and in fuch a crifis it has been always found that the enemies of the nation, however fallen and diftreffed, have obtained hopes, time, and at length vigour to avail themfelves of the weaknefs of a divided government.

Let us then fuppofe that an oppofition is actually formed, but declared to be againft the Minifter, not againft the Sovereign: whenever this is the cafe, perfons not to be mifled by names will with difficulty enter into this diftinction of conduct, but will, I am afraid, confider fuch attempts as dictated at this time by a fpirit of republicanifm too prevalent among us, and that an oppofition to the Minifter is in reality an oppofition meant to the King.

One

One prejudice, my Lord, feems to have coloured almoft all the late political debates in this country, with great detriment to the caufe of truth, the refpect due to the Sovereign, the character of his fervants and the mixed conftitution of Britifh liberty. The prejudice I I mean is the laying it down as a political maxim, taken for granted, that *the Minifter* does every thing, and the King does nothing; an opinion very artfully propagated by men who find it their intereft to oppofe both. I know indeed that by fundamental law the King can do no wrong; becaufe the King cannot act without the advice of his privy council; nor enact without that of his parliament affembled : but I beg leave to infift that the word, *the Minifter*, is a term intirely unknown to our conftitution. It was borrowed, and very improperly borrowed, with many other bad phrafes and bad principles, from France and other arbitrary governments. Moft Princes in fuch governments, either of weak abilities or intirely funk in all the effe-

F   minacy

minacy of pleafure, delegate the charge of public bufinefs to one man only, the Prime Minifter, as he is called, or fubordinate of Royal Authority, who ftands next to the throne, the fole oracle of its counfels, and the channel of all its favours. The Britifh conftitution, formed of three great orders of the State, admits no fuch name as the Minifter, no, not even the title of a Cabinet Counfellor. From the outlines of this fyftem are to be traced many political truths. It is the prerogative of the King of Great Britain to declare war or peace with the advice of his privy council. The right of providing for the charge of either is in the representatives of the people; through them there is a free accefs to the Sovereign for every national grievance to be heard and to be redrefsed, and by them the King has a conftant and open communication with all his fubjects. He has a right to nominate his fervants, the great officers of ftate, who are alfo the fervants of the people, and truftees for the benefit

nefit of both King and people, the falaries of thofe great offices being provided for by parliament.

My Lord, this fhort fketch of our confti-tution is unneceffary indeed to you, but it may be ufeful perhaps to many who have ne-ver thought at all upon the fubject; and the inference I mean to draw from it, is, that under this happy form of government fub-fifting inviolate as it does, confidering the exceeding good intentions of his Majefty, that he has both abilities and inclination to act himfelf at the head of the conftitution, and to be really a King over a free and willing people, no perfons can pretend a high affec-tion and duty to his perfon, and a regard for his family, with any appearance of fince-rity, yet at the fame time endeavour to ren-der unpopular, and even odious, the meafures of the Sovereign under a pretext of any dan-ger to the conftitution, and of running down *the Minifter* only.

F 2

Let

Let it be afked any candid man of a common underftanding, does there appear the leaft
hazard of the liberty, property, and rights
of the people in allowing his Majefty at all
times his own rights too, as well as any
other member of the ftate? Why is he not
to be permitted to chufe his own fervants,
or to difcard them? to be grateful for their
fidelity and activity in the public bufinefs,
and to judge of their inclinations and abilities
for ferving himfelf and his people, and to
honour with his countenance and protection
thofe who merit his favour? I am fure the
condition of a King of Great Britain would
be the moft miferable upon earth, if he were
to be deprived, merely becaufe he is King,
of every comfort a private man holds dear
to his happinefs and interefts; and if it could
be fuppofed that a clamour raifed at any time
by a few diffatisfied perfons refufing to concur
obeying his commands were to deprive him
of the diligence of thofe other fervants who
are willing to obey him, and more efpecially
if,

if, inſtead of being a Prince, he ſhould become at any time a priſoner as it were to his
own ſervants, watched and guarded for their
own purpoſes, that all their miſconduct might
be charged to his account, and all his merits
to theirs. If theſe, my Lord, ſhould ever
be the views of any particular ſet of men,
will they be the real friends of the public or
not? they will not, I think they cannot
deſerve the approbation of the people, or the
favourable reception of their Prince. Nor
will they be able to anſwer for the general
confuſion and diſtreſs occaſioned by their unwarrantable oppoſition, at any time of great
difficulty and danger, when their attempt to
ruin any one ſervant of the King under pre-
tence of ruining the Miniſter will be hazard-
ing in fact the ruin of the ſtate.

My Lord, I have ſaid ſomething before
upon the diſtinctions of general party. Give
me leave to ſay a word upon diſtinctions of
particular perſons. I am ſure you and every

man

man of good fenfe, or indeed of humanity, muft defpife and abhor fuch invidious difcriminations. Did a man's abilities or integrity for the public fervice depend upon the points of the compafs, it would be very right to afk in what degree of latitude or longitude from the great metropolis this man or that man was born? Cornwall or Cumberland, Devonfhire or Dorfetfhire never made a man a better fellow-fubject becaufe he firft drew breath in one of thofe counties, and a geographical diftinction will, I hope, at no time prevent, what it has often promoted, the good fortune of a man of Norfolk, or of Suffex, or of any one town, borough, city, province or divifion in all Great Britain.

I know, my Lord, the honour you have done to the places of your education. Yet I do not believe you are a better or a wifer man merely for an education at Weftminfter. It does not fignify from what great man I take my example. The prefent minifter was bred

from

from a child at Eton, but I dare fay it will be
no motive to him to prefer Eton men for that
reafon: nor do I think it a very important circumftance where his eftate lies; his ftake and
that of his family is nearly as great, upon
Englifh ground, as that of any of the Englifh nobility, and a Scottifh title will only
make him, I believe, my Lord, you think
fo, more tender than any other man would
chufe to be, of the humour prevalent among
the lefs fenfible inhabitants of this ifland,
who delight in diftinctions, and are like their
old Britifh anceftors, *hofpitibus feri*. In the
lower offices of government good proofs
might be brought of a much greater number
of Northern people preferred, and lefs publicly noticed under former adminiftrations,
than under the prefent minifter; and, if there
are any Scottifh or Irifh Lords or common-
ers, now in the great offices of ftate, I believe all the world knows he found them
there.

How-

However, my Lord, I am fure no candid man can object to their being there, except fuch men as find it convenient at different times to enforce or leap over a diftinction juft as it fits their interefts. After all, it is paying no great compliment to the prefent minifter, nor is it any reflexion upon his predeceffors, to fay that he has good underftanding enough as well as they had, not to reject or pre-fer men for patronymics. To fpeak fairly, and, if poffible, to deftroy all diftinctions whatever, let us for once go to the bottom of all of them. I am fure you, my Lord, who are of the moft focial temper poffible, will, above all men, thoroughly hate them, when you confider the principle, which has from the beginning of the world fet men at variance. The whole fecret I have ever taken to be this ill-natured proverb, " the fewer the better chear." A diftinc-tion, a name, it matters not what, ferves at different times the purpofe to keep a few men in, and a great many out of all good things.

things. And from this one fource has flow-
ed the long lift of epithets of party, which
have difhonoured and embroiled religion and
government from the beginning of the world
to the deftruction of all common fenfe and
common honefty. How much is the bulk of
mankind to be pitied, who fuffer their prejudices to be improved in fuch a manner by
a few artful men : who, overturning all the
firft principles of religion and good government, which were meant to unite more
clofely, not to feparate mankind, eftablifh
an undue influence over their fellow-creatures,
which is thus obtained, by fomenting divifions even unto blood? Such is the old maxim
fo often and fo fuccefsfully purfued, divide and
tyrannize.

" But it is right fometimes to oppofe mea-
" fures in a free government, if not the man."
True. Oppofition to meafures in fome cafes
I allow is neceffary, and that the good of the
whole refults frequently from the collifion of

the parts. But then unanimity ought not to be broken merely for the fake of breaking it. Some objections, in order to juftify oppofition, muft be made with colour to the meafures, that they are contrived or conducted weakly or wickedly, or that they proceed from a fpirit of timidity or indecifion.

There have been times in the hiftory of all countries remarkable for this indecifive temper in adminiftrations: when minifters have lived upon the daily bread of their po-litics. Happy to get rid of a prefent incumbrance, or to remedy a prefent inconvenience at the expence of a thoufand future ones.

The defcription drawn by the Duke de Sully of the conduct of the miniftry of Charles IX. of France, and his obfervations upon it, are fo very remarkable, that I beg leave to quote them.

" En matiere d'etat rien n'eft pire que cet
" efprit

" efprit d'indecifion. Il ne faut dans les con-
" jonctures difficiles tout abandonner ni tout
" refufer au hazard, mais après avoir choi-
" fon but par des reflexions fages et froides
" il faut que toutes les demarches qu'on fait
" tendent à y parvenir. On ne fçauroit *en-*
" *core trop acheter ni trop preffer une paix ne-*
" *ceffaire.* Mais ce qu'il faut eviter le plus
" foigneufement dans les circonftances cri-
" tiques, c'eft de tenir les efprits du peuple
" en fufpens entre la paix et la guerre. Ce
" n'etoit pas par de telles maximes que fe
" conduifoit le confeil de Catherine de Me-
" dicis. Si l'on y prenoit un parti, ce n'e-
" toit que pour le moment et jamais pour la
" fin, et c'etoit toûjours dans une maniere fi
" timide qu'on ne remedioit au prefent même
" que tres imparfaitement. Le defaut de
" tous les efprits qui ont plus de vivacité
" que de jugement eft de fe reprefenter ce
" qui eft proche de maniere à s'en laiffer
" eblouir, et de ne voir ce qui eft loin qu'au
" travers d'un nuage. *Quelques momens, quel-*

" *ques*

" *ques jcurs*, voila ce qui compofe pour eux
" l'avenir."

But there is a real ftate of things, as well
as the difpofitions of minifters, which produces delay, timidity and indecifion in public
adminiftrations; I mean unwarrantable oppofitions, my Lord; great and powerful factions
in the ftate, and the condition of the times, and
of a nation not yet fufficiently armed and provided, for the defence of both its extremities,
and its center. A nation, at a certain period,
has flid into an immenfe war of a fudden:
the very moment which has been feized by
foreign enemies to fpread terror and difmay
among the people, has been feized too by
factious fubjects at home, as an opportunity to
difplay their parts, and to figure in an oppofition, for the diftrefling of government. Vanity,
no lefs than avarice, every hour, my Lord,
prompts men to be factious; and times are
remembered, when the leaders of faction have
beat up for volunteers againft government,
and

and vifited with all the humility of ambition
obfcure places to court and bring out men
of active, fiery, and overbearing difpofitions,
of fmall fortunes and great paffions, but poffeffed of abilities that recommend the poffef-
fors to the popular voice, in order to join the
cry; to receive favours firft from government, and then to fly in the face of it. I
need not point out to you, my Lord, facts
of this kind. They will only fhew, that unreafonable and vehement oppofition on one
fide, often produces indecifion on the other;
and that when this is the cafe, all the evils
of it are to be charged to thofe perfons
only, who lay fo terrible a foundation of the
caufe of timidity and indecifion in placing
every obftacle they can poffibly invent in the
way of government.

Men of the beft hearts are often the moft
timid; being tender of their fellow-fubjects
and of human nature, experienced in the
fatal reverfes of all human things, and above
all

all concerned for fear of burfting that which
a touch may burft, the vaft and fwoln bub-
ble of artificial wealth, the credit of a nation,
they may be averfe to entering precipitately
into violent meafures, the beginnings of which
are eafily underftood, but the end of which
is removed beyond the knowledge or con-
jecture of the wifeft of men.

But can timidity or delay or indecifion be
attributed to the prefent meafures of government? Are they to be charged with a hafte
that makes no progrefs, an attention to fub-
alterns who have nothing to recommend them
but the extreme ductility of their character?
is there any jealous fear of adopting plans of
operation likely to require abler men to execute them than thofe who adopt them? is
there difcovered any habitual flutter, or air
of bufinefs, or a vanity of undertaking all
things without doing any, till bufinefs does
itfelf by other hands, or, in the common
courfe of human affairs, fettles into fome point

or

or other by its own natural weight? This is not the cafe, my Lord.

The great perfons who now affift in guiding the reins of government have not turned pale or fainted at fpectres; no not even at that tremendous one of the proud, obftinate, and menacing genius of Iberia. Martinico, the moft important conqueft of all the poffeffions of France in America, is our own; by which France is wounded in the tendereft part of her commerce. The Havannah, the arfenal and citadel of all the Spanifh Weft-Indies, has fubmitted to our arms. Newfoundland is once more ours without a blow. And as to Germany, which has not been neglected, it is the rock againft which France has beaten herfelf in vain. Every thing fpeaks the activity and the integrity of the minifters of his Majefty, who have done their duty by a war which was not their own, and have been guided by the neceffity of prefent circumftances, not by the retrofpect of beginnings.

So

So that no one part of the public fervice has
fuffered upon any pretext whatfoever.

The time, my Lord, is at length arrived

*Quod optanti Divum promittere nemo
Auderet, volvenda dies en attulit ultro.*

when we fee a native Britifh King acting upon
truly Britifh principles: when there is a free
Britifh parliament, if ever there was one:
when it would be doing injuftice to the
popularity and affection which his Majefty
ought amply to poffefs in the hearts of all
his fubjects not to proclaim to the world the
extreme purity of his government; and that
integrity and moderation which will be the
eternal glory of his reign : when in the election
of the reprefentatives of the people, the leaft
bias of office and revenue was ftrictly forbid-
den to be made ufe of in the ftrongeft terms,
" the King will have it fo:" when his
Majefty defires nothing fo much as to know
the true fenfe of his people, and when for
their

their fakes, a late very great Minifter has publicly faid it, he was convinced that his Majefty would even part with the antient patrimony of his houfe, if thofe whofe duty it is to give him advice thought it truly for the general interefts of this nation, that it fhould ceafe having any weight in the empire and on the continent of Europe, in which France has found it at all times fo much her intereft to cultivate an influence at the expence of vaft armies, and enormous fubfidies upon a principle of rivalfhip to Great Britain, and of acquiring frefh power, fubjects, and territory in Europe fufficient to indemnify her for any advantages which this nation may reap, if fuccefsful in other parts of the world, in its maritime capacity only.

What then remains, my Lord? what but, that more than Herculean tafk, to render men wife, equitable, moderate, and good? I need fay very little to you, my Lord, to convince you of the great difficulties a minifter in this country labours under in carrying on a war, and above all, in making a peace. The wafte of men and treafure, the neceffity of frefh fupplies, the deficiency of thofe already granted and expended, the oppreffion of encreafing taxes upon induftrious labour, which in all human probability are never to be removed, the reverfe to which the nature of all human affairs and the moft fuccefsful war is conftantly liable, the fevere judgment formed by mankind of the wifdom and honefty of all meafures, or the contrary, by the good or ill fuccefs of the event only; thefe, my Lord, are all terrifying, very terrifying circumftances to the ableft and beft minifter, however his fyftem of conduct at home or abroad may be well formed, and whether the war in which a nation is involved be in confequence or not of his own counfels or of other men. You, my Lord, who know the internal force of this country better than moft men, have often, I make no doubt, revolved in your mind very ferious confiderations on the occafions which began the

prefent

prefent war, you know what was its object, what may be expected to be its end, and what are the means that were held once, or are now held neceffary to obtain that object, and to bring about that end. How many fears are there that a nation making moft violent efforts at a great diftance from home, and in every other part of the globe, fhould exhauft the force neceffary for its defence in that part where its very exiftence is concerned ? for how many empires have fallen low into debility and contempt by too vehement and too long continued an exertion of the principles by which they firft grew up to ftrength and power ? In carrying on the prefent war, it will be of great importance to confider to what a nice point the paper credit of this nation, both of a public and a private nature, which is equally extenfive, may be ftrained with fafety ; the reflexion will be important, how far the looms may be deferted, at a time when we can fcarce fupply our conquefts, our colonies and ourfelves with neceffary manufac-

tures ;

tures; how long the plough may be neglected, and the flower of our youth continue to perish in the plains of Germany, or of Portugal, or underneath the torrid zone: but above all, will it be a very serious subject of consideration, how far the mother-country, besides the depopulation she suffers from her inhabitants, who thus fall in the very arms of victory a sacrifice to military glory, can sustain the farther depopulation she suffers by the multitudes in every war settling in her colonies; they are well known to encrease in double the number of their inhabitants, with a vast addition of wealth and power from the outset of a long war: a degree of encrease which may one day prove exceedingly dangerous, whenever the necessity of new-modelling the government of the colonies shall rouse, as it will rouse undoubtedly, one day or other, a spirit of independency, that now sleeps unheard of.

This, my Lord, is but a short sketch of the difficul-

difficulties that fall to the heavy lot of the immediate fervants of the Sovereign : they are indeed difficulties which arife from the general nature of government, and the circumftances of the war. But there are other difficulties which arife elfewhere, and which may grow bigger, or diminifh, as faction or ignorance, or good fenfe and candour fhall prevail among thofe, whofe duty it is to execute and obey.

What difficulties can be greater than thofe which arife from the temper and prejudices of a free people? To preach chaftity to a young and paffionate lover, who holds a beautiful miftrefs in his arms, or ferioufnefs and fobriety to a bonvivant already heated with champagne, would be efteemed a fruitlefs and even a ridiculous attempt. But how much more arduous and even hopelefs is the labour to moderate the paffions, the avidity and ambition of numbers, who are capable of making themfelves of confequence

to

to government, by an ability and inclination at leaft, to do a great deal of mifchief, if they are not kept fufficiently in humour to do a very little good? and above all, how hard is it to fatisfy a general thirft of conqueft, a fury of dominion unnatural, but becoming habitual to a commercial people?

A nation inflamed under fuch circumftances, to whom it may be faid truly, what Demofthenes faid to the Athenians, *" your " orators have fpoiled you,"* is not eafily brought off from the vifionary fchemes of glory, which an excefs of adulation has long prefented to its view. From the fpeaker in the fenate to the writer of a news-paper in the garret, there feems to be but one view, to ftudy the difpofition of fuch a people, to follow, not to lead it; for whatever the political difeafe happens to be, thefe ftate empirics are fure to recommend nothing but what they firft find is perfectly agreeable to their patients, notwithftanding that fuch a treatment of their difor-

der

der is pernicious, and tends only to encreafe the malady. In other words, a nation is to be ruined, that a news-paper may fell.

My Lord, it is with whole nations as it is with private men; an accumulation of poffef-fions only' ferves to increafe a violent defire for ftill greater acquifitions. Every conqueft opens new views; and the imagination already grafps the mines of Chili, Peru, and Mexico. What fubjects for declamation! every voice and every pen is employed to increafe the national rage of perpetuating war: and by a thirft of military glory we feem to have intirely forgot that moderation and equity which always gave this nation the greateft weight in Europe, becaufe hitherto her object was to preferve the peace and liberties of its neighbours inviolate, to excite no jealoufies, to crufh every attempt of any greater power for the intire conquering or dividing the dominions of any minor potentate; and to obtain over the minds of other nations by equity that univerfal em-

empire which Louis XIV. attempted in vain
by the force of fleets and armies. Un-
fortunately for that Prince, the writers of
his nation, more than even his courtiers, fo-
mented his paffion for military exploits by an
excefs of adulation; and the extreme miferies
which France fuffered in the end from that
warlike fpirit muft be placed in a very great
degree to their account, fo terrible was the
effect which the flatteries of thofe oracles of
the people had in victorious times upon the
fpirit of their Sovereign and of their fellow-
fubjects.   May not the fame cafe unhappily
become that of a free nation, which, dazzled
with the glorious blaze of heroic fentiments,
may be induced to overlook the juft point
where to leave off and fheath the fword, but
to be refolved, like the monarch of Epirus,
not to fit down and be happy till another
and another conqueft fhall be added to the former without limits ?

With refpect to the conquefts which we
have

have already made with fuch unparalleled
fuccefs, are we not already embarraffed how to
preferve them? nor am I fure that it is our
intereft to retain them.

The beft writers of all countries, upon the
fubject of commerce and of the interefts of
Europe, feem to have agreed that the wealth
of the American world can never be in better
hands than in thofe of the Spanifh nation : inafmuch as bullion is the means of wealth to other
nations, but is not really wealth itfelf, being only the vehicle for interchanging the produce of
induftry. It is the number of people, the induftry, the valour, the fpirit of a nation, which
conftitute the real wealth of it, and in fuch
refpects bullion is not intrinfically more valuable than paper, leather, the iron rings of
the Lacedemonians, or the fhells called cou-
ryes, which are ufed for traffic by Eaftern
nations. What beggary, what pride, what
indolence, what depopulation to Spain, has
been derived from her mines of gold and fil-

ver? No fooner does the fleet, laden with the wealth of America, arrive, than this vaft mafs of bullion quits the royal treafury and circulates all over Europe with rapidity to pay for com- modities even neceffary for the fuftenance of life to the inhabitants of Spain, which other induftrious nations poffefs over and above their own confumption. What then might be the confequence of the mines of America being annexed for ever to the poffeffions of Great Britain is a fubject which for my own part I confider with terror: already are we vitiated fufficiently by our commerce, and fhall doubt-lefs perifh by the means of that very commerce which has made us great. Whoever remem-bers the effect which the mere expectation of the South-feas being opened in a very fmall degree to the Britifh nation had upon the minds of the people, from the confufion, the excefs, the madnefs of thofe times, may eafily form an idea of the effect which the intire and actual poffeflion of all the wealth of the American mines would have upon the

man-

manners of this people. In fuch a fituation the world's victors would be fubdued very foon by their own vices. Luxury, profufion, and the want of every principle of good government and fubordination in all orders of men would bring on effeminacy, indolence, depopulation, and all the wretched train of mifery that accompanies the degeneracy of every great nation. Spain, before the difcovery of the Indies, was full of people, brave and free. What fhe is now, our fuccefs has fhewn us, weak, contemptible, and vulnerable in every part. If therefore we have any defire to preferve to our country all that is dear to it, and can make it wife, moderate, virtuous and happy, let us not indulge the avarice of a few particular men; and I hope never to fee a war carried on, or a pacification made, upon principles *folely* mercantile, or which are dictated by a fpirit of funding. What muft be the war, what muft be the peace of a nation of ftockjobbers?

I ex-

I except merchants, who are truly fo, men of real property and honour, but to fuch a fort of men as thefe are who fport with the properties of us all, it would hardly be too coarfe to fay in the language of Shakefpear's tribune to the Roman rabble bawling at his heels, " Out, hang, ye dogs, ye like nor war " nor peace." But if any faction can be pernicious in a ftate, it is a faction of merchants. Men nurfed in the narrow paths of life, incapable even of forming any extenfive ideas of general commerce, but only reafoning from thofe acquired by them in a particular corner of the vaft complicated machine of human intercourfe in the change of property, are certainly very ill judges of the great intereft of nations, refpecting their internal and external forces, and the relation they bear to the reft of the powers of Europe with which they are furrounded.

There is alfo another objection to the opinions of mercantile men prevailing in the govern-

government of a kingdom. Merchants are so little in fact the subjects of any one nation, that the law of nations has very properly confidered them as divefted of their original national character, by their occafional and frequent adoptions of another character from time to time taken, as it fuits their intereft, from the place of their refidence, where they are faid to be domiciled for the purpofes of trade. Thus an Engiiſh merchant in France is confidered as a Frenchman, and a Frenchman refident in England as an Engliſhman. They form a kind of republic in the heart of all countries, independent of the places of their birth, and their connections even with that very government under the protection of which they refide are extremely weak.

Thus, in the midft of the moft general war, there is a chain of mercantile interefts running through the midft of the belligerant kingdoms, and linking in very clofe fociety men, who, as natives and vaffals of this or

that

that Sovereign, are fuppofed to be in the utmoft enmity poffible. Laudable indeed is this fyftem of humanity, that counteracts fo happily the cruelty of the divifions that arife from the ambition of princes, and which ferves to fufpend and mitigate the rigours of war, the fcourge of human nature. But merchants muft not fet up for the governors of kingdoms.

Although in details of any particular branch of commerce mercantile men are to be heard, and even fought for and con-fulted, it is the exalted bufinefs of fuperior minds to draw general conclufions from the complex of national interefts, and to place the glory, power, and profperity of a country upon an extenfive, folid, and lafting bafis. Here is the great province of a firm and en-lightened minifter; and upon fuch a fubject it will require no little courage to withftand the avarice of particular men, when the glory of a nation feems united in a common caufe of defir-

ing

ing to retain a perpetuity without limits in dominions newly acquired by victorious arms.
It is no wonder, if in the midst of conquests,
and the founds of triumph, the still small voice
of deep thought and peaceful meditation cannot be heard, which reprefents with forrow the
weaknefs, the mifery of even the moft fuccefsful conquerors, the depopulation of kingdoms, and the effufion of human blood,
poured forth like water over the face of the
whole earth.

Were we to indulge defcription upon this
fubject, how terrible a picture would the
prefent general war offer to the eyes of men?
Happy as our own nation has been, in the
courfe of it, yet what numerous, and once re-
fpectable families among us have funk into extreme indigence from the fudden fluctuations
of property? It is a very alarming confideration, when we think of the great decreafe of the
value of the capital ftock of the feveral public
funds, decreafing in proportion to the additional
ftock

ftock created upon every new loan in every
year of the war, to fo prodigious an amount,
and fo much to the prejudice of the antient
creditors ofthe public, the fupporters of government and the proteftant eftablifhment, in the
worft of times. It is very painful to reflect upon
the encreafe of taxes upon all the neceffary arti-
cles of life, and even upon our own manufactures themfelves, befides the number of taxes
running almoft in a circle, fo that they tread upon one another, inafmuch as the fame things
feem to be taxed more than once; befides the
revenue of them being mortgaged in fuch a
manner, that there are no probable hopes of
their ceafing, but by paying off, or annihilat-
ing the capital to which they are deftined for
the intereft ; and that above all, how terrible
is the confideration that a whole nation living like a private man upon its principal, muft,
of neceffity, like a private man at laft put a
ftop to its payments ! The vifible decreafe of
people in two wars fo near each other in
point of time, is alfo a very ftriking reflection

tion to thofe who obferve what children, old, and decrepit men have been taken into our late levies of new troops, by which great numbers of officers have been created at a prodigious expence, when it was thought more expedient by fome very intelligent commanders to recruit perfectly the old corps. Nothing is fo apparent as the monopolizing fpirit of trade, availing itfelf of the prefent demands of government in fo high a degree as to create diftrefs of the common neceffaries of life in the midft of abundance. The want of hands in all our manufactures, the almoft impoffibility of procuring them in the bufineffes of building and hufbandry, are all painful facts, and too generally felt for it not to be confeffed, that the efforts of this nation have already brought on weakneffes upon it which will require great time, attentention, and wifdom to remedy. Were it poffible for Great Britain to put out both eyes of France, fhe muft lofe one of her own. And I am inclined to think that a balance

K   of

of commerce in a certain degree, may be as
ufeful and neceffary to England, and. to the
reft of the nations of Europe, as a balance of
power ; fince each nation ought to. have
fomething left to interchange with another;
otherwife were it poffible that one fhould
grafp the whole of commerce, and the reft
be left bare as the wild favages of America,
where would be that commutation, that cir-
culation of property, the great fources of induftry, which conftitute the happinefs of in-
dividuals, and the real intereft of every nation as a diftinct fociety ? Thefe difficulties,
thefe evils then, which I have mentioned, will
fall to the painful lot of the minifter who
fhall make a peace for this nation. Other
men will bear the glories of its conquefts, and
exult in its treafures ; he only muft heal the
wounds, fupport the falling, build up again
the fallen parts, reunite the divided, and
ftrengthen the whole of government. It is
undoubtedly much eafier to carry on the war,
and to follow the general bent of popular inclinations,

clinations, as it is eafier to pufh a vaft weight
rolling down the hill with an encreafing velo-
city, than to urge it up with labour to its
fummit, and fix it there upon a folid bafis.
Greater therefore will be the obligations of
this country to the man, who fhall difentan-
gle the complicated interefts of the feveral
powers at war, and provide for the prefent
honour, and future fafety of the nation at this
crifis, than to all the minifters who have un-
dertaken before in any period the reins of a
Britifh adminiftration. But how little can it
be expected, my Lord, that fuch a bufinefs
will be compleated with fuccefs, if the hands
of the Sovereign or his fervants are not left
at perfect liberty, fo that their abilities and
their integrity, their zeal for the public good,
may have a fair and open field left for their
utmoft exertion? Were it poffible to conceive
that there fhould exift any faction in the ftate
equally defirous of pacification, yet that fuch
a faction fhould be determined to ruin, if
poffible, a bufinefs of fo much difficulty in

K 2

its

its own nature, becaufe it is not its own work, or to hunt the maker of it down hereafter, as a victim to public difcontent, for imperfections of which that very faction was the caufe, fuch a fituation of a kingdom would be confidered by all good men as deplorable in the higheft degree.

Befides all this, my Lord, were the immoderate expectations of mankind no bar to the fuccefs of a minifter in forming a plan of pacification at the fame time that he is pufhing on of neceffity a war in its utmoft extent, yet fo foon as a peace being compleated fhould give an opportunity to redrefs all thofe abufes in offices, which, in proportion to the neceffities of fuch difficult times, ever did and ever will creep into all governments, the uneafinefs occafioned by reforming fuch abufes to thofe who fuffer by the reformation, will take a thoufand colours, and load the head of the minifter with vengeance from every quarter. The very expectation of fuch

re-

reformations taking place as the suppofed confequence of a peace is almoft fufficient to arm
every commander, contractor, monopolizer,
commiffary, and every dependent of office
againft it immediately.

It is very remarkable in the celebrated
memoirs of the Duke de Sully, that when
that great minifter attempted to regulate the
exceffive abufes inveterately rooted in the
French government, and which were the
fources of all its debility, there was fcarcely
a commiffioner in any one department that
did not boldly unite to embarrafs the bufinefs
of the King; the Duke d'Epernon, irritated
to the laft degree, fent a challenge to Sully,
the effect of which was only prevented by
Henry IV. faying publicly, " that if they
fought, he would be Sully's fecond;" at laft
the cabals againft Sully rofe fo high in the
court, that the King, befieged by the faction
of Sully's enemies, advifed him to take care,
for that though he would ftand by him as
long

long as he could, yet if he made one flip, his ruin was inevitably determined. So hard it is, my Lord, for a man of acknowledged integrity and abilities to act upon real principles of fidelity to his prince and country, without braving the utmoft abufe, oppofition, and even revengeful attacks.

But is it not fingular, my Lord, that the beft men at the head of all governments have been attacked, at one time or other of their lives, in this manner, without any plaufible reafons given for the violent oppofition made to their meafures?

Thus, my Lord, you muft be very fenfible, at the prefent crifis, what a clamour, with the utmoft degree of virulence, has been raifed againft a fingle perfon; and I do not know that one better reafon has been offered for that clamour among the general body of the people, than that of the ill-tempered and ignorant Athenian citizen to Ariftides himfelf

for

for the banifhment of him, " that he did not know him, and did not like him."

When therefore no objection can be taken from any thing known and proved againft a great man, fomething muft be faid ; and any thing may be faid, to fupport the views of a faction. There is a very ftriking inftance of this artifice in the infancy of the Roman republic. Junius Brutus, as it is fufpected, entertained fome jealoufy of his fellow conful fharing in the glory of that eftablifhment. The character of Brutus, who was bred in the court of Tarquin, and who, while he remained in it, artfully affected the manners of an idiot, appears to have been that of a very fubtle courtier : his firft ftep, after the e-ftablifhment of the new government, was to in-finuate among the multitude that his colleague, Tarquinius Collatinus, being of a diftant branch of the abdicated monarch, was not a fafe perfon to be intrufted with power. The bulk of mankind generally talk one after another ; and

the

the multitude, as ufual, caught the word " *A Tarquinian*" from their leaders. All the principal perfons in the ftate entered into the views of Brutus. Brutus at length harangued his colleague before the people: he recited the hiftory of the Tarquin family, the danger of it to the revolution, and liberty of the people, and concluded the whole with faying, *Aufer hinc nomen tuum; non placere nomen*. Collatinus, who bore an admirable chara&ter in private and in public life, being of a mild and timid difpofition, yielded to the fa&ion which he faw was powerfully turned againft him, and laid down the fafces, becaufe his *name* was not agreeable to the people; or rather becaufe his virtues were not agreeable to Brutus.

Such are the unhappy effe&ts of an excefs of emulation in every free ftate, which often lofes the joint affiftance of the beft citizens in its greateft neceffities, from an incompatibility of their manners, and too great a degree of ambition to be alone in authority.   I

I believe, my Lord, you will allow that the prejudging of public meafures before they are known, or attempting to dictate them, is another great difficulty to minifters; a practice neither very prudent in itfelf, nor very confiftent with the conftitution. Every act of that kind in any corporate body other than by way of petition to parliament, and through that conftitutional channel up to the throne, does greatly tend to diftrefs government in critical times. In fuch times it is very dangerous to create and introduce a fourth eftate, as it were, of a democratical kind into the conftitution, and which is therefore more liable in its nature to be played off as an engine againft government by the arts of any able fet of men who have a private intereft in inflaming others not quite fo wife as themfelves, and which engine the enemies of a nation may have power to make ufe of no lefs than factious fubjects. " L'aveuglement des " bien intentionnez", which was the cafe of many men in England in the time of

L Charles

Charles I. fays the very fenfible Cardinal de
Retz, who underftood the game of a faction
as well as any man who ever headed one in
any country, " eft fuivi pour l'ordinaire bien-
" tôt après de la penetration de ceux qui mê-
" lent la paffion et la faction dans les interêts
" publics, et qui voyent le futur et le poffible,
" dans le tems que les compagnies reglées ne
" fongent qu'au prefent et l'apparent."

Even the feeking a redrefs of grievances,
my Lord, out of the regular channel of ap-
plication, I apprehend ought to be carefully
avoided by every man who wifhes to preferve
the form of our admirable conftitution, which
fhould be, like the ark of Ifrael, inviolable
and untouched; but the dictation of meafures
from corporate bodies to the throne much
more fo ought to be avoided, as it tends to
deftroy fubordination of every kind, and feems
to be as much an encroachment upon the
rights of parliament to reprefent the complex
fenfe of the nation, as upon the conftitutional
powers of the crown.   From

From the levelling principles in the general
civil war of Charles I. which branched out
into fuch various fets of men, all of which
ftruggled hard to govern the kingdom in their
own way, fprung up at laft the neceffity of
one power to govern all, without controul,
under Cromwell : and the dread of the fame
effects of anarchy or arbitrary power at any
future period, from the fame kind of caufes,
fhould make every good and wife man exert
himfelf, whenever he can, to difcourage the
increafe of any unparliamentary force in the
ftate. The city of London is therefore greatly
to be applauded, that, in its late addrefs to
his Majefty, it has fhewn fo much wifdom,
coolnefs, and moderation. It may indeed
have difappointed many warm unthinking,
but well-meaning men, who wifhed perhaps
to have heard the citizens of London in-
ftructing the throne, and affuming even the
rights of Sovereignty. I dare fay that the
city of London will have no reafon to repent
of its more laudable conduct, and that it may

very fafely rely on his Majefty's undoubted watchfulnefs over the true interefts of all his people. Whereas every act that tends to create diffidence, diftruft, and jealoufy between his Majefty and his people, can only be the moft agreeable circumftance poffible to the inveterate enemies of both.

It is an unhappinefs, and a very great difcouragement, my Lord, to every perfon in the execution of his duty in high offices in a free government, that every little retailer of politics expects to have the various plans, nay even the very *fanctum fanctorum* of government, laid open and juftified to the eyes of prying multitudes at home, and of courfe to the enemies of the ftate abroad, in order that a few talking idle men may be able to figure in their little fenates, and fit attentive to their own applaufes in judgment upon thofe who fhould be their governors. The great, the immortal Scipio, who crufhed the rival of the Roman power, complained to the fenate

in

in the fevereft terms juft before he fet out upon
the expedition againft Carthage, of the bad
effects which thefe minute critics of the ftate
occafioned; while they ruined the reputation
of the ableft men of Rome, and fpread from
barbers fhops, and from other houfes of in-
dolent refort, and the walks upon the forum,
by falfe reports infamy upon government,
difcontent, and even fedition into every corner of the Roman empire.

Popular opinions, my Lord, may be too
much defpifed and neglected. Thofe at the
head of government, who have thought they
always ought to be fo, have fometimes fuffered
for that affectation of indifference; and whoever therefore attempts to direct the violent
current of popular opinions into their due
channel of truth, with candor and integrity,
I believe you will be pleafed to think, does
fome little fervice to his country. In the
language of one of the Claffics, whom I am
the more liberal and frequent in quoting,
well

well knowing your refpect for them, *Nec enim is folus reipublicæ prodeft qui candidatos extrahit et tuetur reos, fed qui juventutem exhortatur, qui in tanta bonorum præceptorum inopia virtute inftruit animos, qui ad pecuniam luxuriamque curfu ruentes, prenfat ac retrahit, et fi nihil aliud, certe moratur.* How much, my Lord, and how ufefully your example and your fentiments will have an influence upon the opinions and conduct of others I need not repeat; for if any man is fenfible, you, my Lord, of all men, are fenfible how hard a tafk it is to prefide in the counfels of a ftate where thofe counfels muft take a conftant bias from the condition of it, which in this kingdom is that of immenfe opulence in particulars, and great indigence in the general; where every exceedingly rich family is of courfe a faction; every able man's luxury and want a fpur to his oppofition, and every the leaft ill fuccefs is the difmay of a wealthy, difcontented, uncertain and jealous people, as eafily depreffed, as it is often immoderately elevated.

Much

Much therefore ought to be allowed to thofe who are called to the moft arduous tafk of affifting their Sovereign in the bufinefs of government.

In this view there is one point, which I ought materially to obferve with refpect to the fituation of any immediate fervant of the crown, whoever he is now or fhall be hereafter, and to whom the principal bufinefs of executing the plan of pacification fhall be delegated at this crifis by the authority of the crown, or in cafe of its failure the province of carrying on the plan of the war.

The point I mean is, my Lord, that it is abfolutely neceffary for the public fervice, if ever we are to have a peace, that as full powers fhould be indulged to the minifter of the peace, whoever he fhall be, as have been allowed to the minifter of the war. By this means the latter has proved fuccefsful beyond our moft fanguine expectations, and by this

means

means the former only can be expected to be
obtained with honour, utility and permanency.
When I faid the minifter of the war, I meant
the late minifter of it ; for hitherto the war
has been carried on with the fame fpirit as
that which firft roufed this nation from its lan-
guor; the arm of power ftretched forth with
all the whole collected force of thefe kingdoms has not been withdrawn or relaxed,
nor has the plan of conducting the war, in order to procure a peace, been bolftered up with
temporary expedients, that weak and worn-
out fupport of lame and impotent politics.
Nothing has been cramped, nothing unfup-
plied; nor can we make the leaft doubt of the
fame tenor of conduct being ftill maintained
with the utmoft refolution by thofe perfons
who have the honour to advife his Majefty at
this time, if the fpirit of levity, prevarication,
and fineffe fhould difcover itfelf as ufual on
the part of France in the courfe of any negotiations for peace. His Majefty knows
what is due to his own dignity, and to the in-

tegrity

tegrity and moderation which he has fhewed to his enemies and the world. In the mean time nothing can tend more to make this nation happy, either in the continuance of a juft and neceffary war, or in fixing a plan of general pacification, than that thofe great perfons, whofe province it is to conduct both the one and the other, fhould meet with no difficulties from any oppofition at home; the advantage of which oppofition can only refult to the general enemy, who will undoubtedly rife in his demands from time to time upon the Britifh miniftry in proportion as he finds them embarraffed by any violent obftacles placed in their way at home.

The early precautions taken, my Lord, the plans purfued, and moft fuccefsfully executed with regard to the Spanifh war, are an unanfwerable proof how very fincere and upright were the fentiments of thofe fervants of his Majefty, who differed with another great man in their opinions of the real intentions

M   of

of Spain. It is to be lamented that the warmth of his temper, the confcioufnefs of his own vaft powers, and a degree of enthufiafm natural to every fuperior mind, induced him at fo very difficult a crifis to withdraw from his Sovereign, and his country, his fervices fo acceptable and even fo neceffary to both, and to confider his own honour fo deeply interefted as he confidered it, not in any difference of opinion about the meafure in general, but about the point of timing it, and the expecting only the return of a courier with the pofitive anfwer of the Spanifh court.

The event, my Lord, feems to have fhewed that the interefts of this nation have not been at all prejudiced by the delay of the meafure of the Spanifh war; for it was certainly an advantage that the Britifh fubjects in Spain in confequence of that delay gained time to fettle their affairs there, and to remove themfelves and their effects; for had this government attacked fo punctilious a nation, and fo vindictive as Spain is, without any obfervance of the law of nations, this impetuofity might have been attended with confequences very dangerous to the properties, and perhaps to the perfons of all the Britifh fubjects refident in that country.

Inafmuch as the meafures with regard to Spain have now fucceeded, the backwardnefs fhewed by the Britifh nation to commence hoftilities will prove no fmall means towards facilitating a peace with that power, or extending ftill farther our conquefts over its colonies, as it furnifhes the moft convincing proof poffible to the whole Spanifh nation, that Great Britain conquers unwillingly, and feels the utmoft concern for a people, whofe natural interefts fhe efteems as her own. While our arms are thus exerted, neither with a fpirit of avarice, revenge or ambition, we may expect the fame continuance of extenfive fuccefs as we have hitherto enjoyed,

and

and the fame folidity of influence, whenever
our arms fhall be laid down, over the reft of
Europe. The opinion which the fubjects of
all other nations will entertain of the advantages experienced by entering into our alliance,
or becoming united to us as fellow-fubjects,
their ideas of our equity and moderation will
fupport the power we have obtained by the
force of fleets and armies, when thofe violent
means fhall be no longer exerted. Thus the
virtues of old Rome fubdued more of her
enemies, than even her firm legionary vete-
rans, and victorious eagles: and I hope, my
Lord, that we fhall be able to apply to our
own country the fame glorious eulogium as was
addreffed to the immortal genius of that great
republic,

Dis te minorem quod geris imperas.

I have preffed, my Lord, and I am forry that the difpofitions of the times make it
fo very proper for me to prefs again the importance and neceffity of full powers at this
crifis

crifis being allowed to the fervants of his Majefty, whoever they are or may be. I would detract from no man's merit in conducting a war or carrying on a negotiation. It is no detraction from the aftonifhing abilities of the Sovereign of Pruffia, to fay that his fuccefs furpaffing the bounds of all human expectation, is owing under providence to the uncontrollable power he poffeffes as an abfolute Sovereign at the head of his people and his armies; as the ear, the eye, the informing fpirit of the collected force of all his fubjects. It is well known, that the fuccefs of the Duke of Marlborough, that able ftatefman as well as foldier, both with regard to war and peace, would have been much greater than it was, had not the Dutch deputies cramped his operations of the one in the field, and a faction at home the other in the council. Many French generals have failed in undertakings of the higheft importance, by being fettered with plans formed not in the camp and upon the fcene of action, but in the cabinets of priefts, women,

women, or ftatefmen fprung from the robe, who neither heard, faw, or underftood what was really expedient. But there is no need to point out, my Lord, what fatal difadvantages in all ages and countries have attended the execution of any bufinefs of a public nature, in which the utmoft difficulties are to be furmounted, when the commiffion has been cramped by narrow powers.

If then the work of a pacification, fuch as fhall give peace to all the nations in Europe, fuch as fhall cut off the fources of a future war, by leaving nothing undecided, and fhall provide effectually for the fecurity of this country, and obtain all the firft objects of the conteft, and a very ample indemnification for its own damages, and for thofe of its unhappy allies who have groaned under the fevereft fcourge of the moft calamitous perfecution, for the fake of this country only; if I fay this work, my Lord, is arduous beyond meafure, nay attended with fuch difficulties, that nothing but con-

confummate wifdom, integrity, and perfever-
ance can furmount them, beyond the analogy
of every war, then I afk, does it not become
every honeft man to join all hearts and hands
to leffen thofe difficulties as much as poffible,
and to pufh the veffel into port?

The obfervations I have juft now made
will fhow, my Lord, that I mean not to leffen the obligations we all have, and fhame
be to thofe who think we have none, to a man,
who undertook to guide the veffel in its greateft danger, with the utmoft courage and in-
trepidity, when I fay that it was fomething
towards his particular fuccefs, that he plan-
ned, advifed, and executed without contra-
diction, that he borrowed the majority of
others, to ufe his own expreffion, and that
he was fuffered to carry every thing his own
length, and quite in his own way. This was
an indulgence certainly uncommon in a free
ftate, and which his enemies expected in fo
warm a man would have proved his ruin, by
fome

fome great difappointment, or by making him fcarce mafter of his temper, by too much fuccefs. Hiftory is full of examples that encouraged fuch expectations. To an excefs of power and confidence of enterprize were owing the fate of the famous author of the revolution at Naples, and the King of Pruffia's misfortunes after the victory of Prague.

An unbounded power was neceffary in this country to be invefted in a fingle man under the preffing and terrible circumftances of the times I allude to. You thought it fo, my Lord, and had weight enough with your Sovereign to make him think fo too; your entreaties, your tears, it is faid, prevailed. Like another Dictator of the Roman ftate, in times of uncommon danger armed with the force of a *fenatus confultum, ne quid detrimenti caperet refpublica,* one man almoft alone affumed the whole power of Britifh government in the conduct of the war, and was fuccefsful; fuccefsful beyond our moft fanguine hopes, and

and the wifhes of his own enemies, and of the enemies of his country.

It is with pain I recall to mind the general depreffion, the panic of this nation at that time. What weaknefs, what uncertainty, what trepidation in the ftate! what alarms, what clamours, what difcontent, divifions, and diftrefs were heard and feen among particulars! Thanks, my Lord, to that great man, and thanks to your Grace for fupporting him; a fpirit of concord, of determination was raifed in this country and government, which fixed its conduct, roufed it from its indecifion and flumber, and has crowned it with unparalleled fucceffes in every part of the globe.

But, my Lord, inafmuch as the unravelling and winding up the whole is more important and difficult than drawing out the clue, I apprehend the propofition to be clearly eftablifhed, that the prefent crifis demands a Dictator of peace as well as there has been one of war: I only wifh the duty which remains to be difcharged were equally adapted to pleafe and fatisfy the views of all men; and that the path to be trod now were as eafy to find and to be trod, as that which has been trod before; and that it were unembarraffed with thorns, and fimple in its purfuit; a path, which fo few men even of the greateft courage, and even of the greateft popularity too I may venture to fay, dare to tread. Yet I hope no man's intereft in fame or power will fo far direct his conduct at this awful crifis, when the Divine Providence has put into the hands of this nation the ballance of its fate between itfelf and its enemies, as to induce him to refufe lending his affiftance to preferve unanimity and mutual confidence amongft us.

How many men, I fear, my Lord, for their own fakes, will fhrink from touching that enormous weight of public interefts which has long been labouring up the fteep of every
diffi-

difficulty, and is nearly placed upon its fummit, to fix there for ever the glory and
felicity of the Britifh nation on a folid bafis.
Our want of unanimity alone can occafion
this vaft weight to recoil upon us to our
deftruction; and whoever the man fhall be,
I care not who he is, who fhall effect fo
amazing a work, will deferve from his country, and from a more grateful pofterity, the
higheft honours that can be paid to a mortal
being.

I think, my Lord, I need fay no more to
you upon this head who are fo well convinced
of the neceffity and foundation of thefe great
and folemn truths; to you, my Lord, who have
it fo much in your power, and, I flatter myfelf, fo very much in your inclination, to ftand
forth in thefe times of intemperate heats and
miftaken difcontents, prejudices, and faction,
the *vir pietate gravis et meritis* I have
placed for my motto; to reconcile, to allay,
and to unite.

But,

But, my Lord, inafmuch as, in order to attain the falutary end of a general cooperation of all orders of men, the good fenfe of the body of the people of Great Britain muft be firft informed and convinced as well as declaimed to, before we can hope that they will diveft themfelves of any vehement prejudices, which they have either formed by the natural difpofitions of mankind, or which they have learnt from their mafters in politics, upon the fubject of the general meafures of his Majefty; and as my intention is to comprehend every thing that may juftify them at all times fo far as they are undoubtedly juftifiable, I will endeavour to point out, as well as I can, the poffibilities and probabilities attending the mixed interefts of this nation at home and abroad, as they are underftood to be, at this particular period: a wide field of matter indeed it may feem, but I humbly apprehend laying in a very narrow compafs.

I con-

I conceive that it is the more neceſſary to enter upon a detail of the principles of the war, becauſe they muſt operate upon the principles of a peace, or the manner of continuing the war for the future.

Whoever looks back to the peace of Aix la Chapelle will ſee in that indeciſive peace the whole object of the preſent war. The great hiſtorian of that part of the late war which was in Italy, but, ſpeaking of the war in general, gives the character of that peace in very ſtriking terms : " Illud hujuſce bel-
" li de quo ſcribimus præcipuum eſt, quòd
" tot præliis tot cladibus, tantorumque Re-
" gum viribus nihil pæne perfectum eſt, quod
" rerum magnitudini reſponderit, non princi-
" pum ambitio ſedata, non populorum ſta-
" bilita felicitas; bellum denique vehemens
" atque atrox pax repente concluſerit otioſis
" magis optanda et defatigatis neceſſaria quam
" cuiquam opportuna aut glorioſa bellantium."

There

There is no doubt but the leaving in the treaty of Aix la Chapelle the American limits to future conferences fowed all the feeds of the prefent war; and therefore almoft all men of reflection forefaw what has fince happened, and confidered that pacification as little better than a truce. I am afraid indeed few definitive treaties as they are called are much better. France faw the peace of Aix la Chapelle in this light, and proceeded wifely enough; her principle was very fimple; fhe thought it for her intereft, that England fhould truft her, and fhe not truft England; and therefore difhonoured this nation by a demand of hoftages which were granted. In the mean time France remained armed, and repaired her navy, encouraged the Indians to moleft the back fettlements of the Britifh colonies, while this nation laid up its fhips, reduced the number of its troops and artificers, who took refuge in France and Spain. As if the treaty had been definitive in fact as well as in words, occupied totally with reducing the

load

load of public credit, that there might be fomething to mortgage in a future war, and attending to a few favings, the Britifh minifters feemed determined to contend no more during their power, if poffible, with France, concerning which they believed, or had argued themfelves and half the nation into a belief of it, that France was too wife, too brave, too much every thing that is great and powerful for this nation to ftruggle with. Yet the minifters of that time had great merit, my Lord: but their pacific fentiments encouraged the enterprizing temper of the French government, whofe levity and ignorance of the internal of this country, from their contempt of it, has always been remarkable: they openly fitted out a fleet, embarked troops, built forts on our territories, difregarded all reprefentations, and defied the Britifh minifters, till they provoked the Britifh nation. They looked upon the preparations for war in England as a parade meant only to amufe the people: but which certainly

tainly inflamed them. The war broke out in America: it was impoffible for the reft of Europe to look on, and fee the two dominant powers, who give the tone to the reft of their neighbours, thus furioufly engage, without expecting the ftorm to fall upon the continent. All was foon in motion there: treaties offenfive and defenfive were made ; old foes became new allies ; and very folemn engagements were entered into to keep thofe out, whom engagements juft before had been entered into to bring in. In a word, France expected that fhe could play a fure card in Europe, and probably gain fomething in America. She knew fomebody would fall upon Hanover. If England fupported the Houfe of Auftria againft Pruffia, fhe imagined the latter would fill Hanover with its troops; as a great traveller at that time has obferved, in his account publifhed of that country, it was in the King of Pruffia's power to do in four and twenty hours. If England fupported Pruffia, fhe determined to

fall

fall upon Hanover herfelf. She knew, how-ever the Englifh nation might be averfe to continental meafures, that nevertheless it has always been, and always muft be obliged to keep pace with every ftep France pleafes to take upon the continent, for fear of her en-creafing her territory and influence with fo much danger to England, and gaining an extent of coaft fo exceffively formidable as France might do from Bayonne to the Zuyder Zee, if England did not interpofe; befides, fhe knew that a nation which acts upon the defen-five muft follow and fight its opponent upon fuch ground as the nation chufes which attacks.

Thus, my Lord, were we foon drawn upon the continent in fpite of all oppofition at home. Auftria refufed to fave Hanover, if England would not depart from its folemn guarantee of Silefia, and if England did depart from it, Hanover would have fallen probably a facrifice to Pruffia, in revenge for a breach of public faith. France thought that the fufferings of

O Hanover

Hanover would pay for America at the worft of events; fhe therefore openly declared her intentions, and joined with the houfe of Auftria: the latter appeared ready to make a facrifice abfolutely of all the Netherlands, if France would enable her to afford it, and fhe was willing to pledge them into her hands for the prefent, in order that fhe might round her dominions again by recovering Silefia. Thus France faw her great object, and the dread of England, the whole Netherlands hypothecated, and as good as given up to her: fhe faw too Holland awed, and at her commands ready to affift her by a neutrality more ufeful than a declaration in the favour of France and her allies.

The imagination of Auftria already grafped all the dominions of the lefs powers on the other fide of the Rhine, and France hoped for all on this fide. The armies of France marched into Germany: and when England undertook to defend Hanover, a great man at
home

home oppofed it; he thought the engagement
to defend Hanover would make it of fo much
the more confequence in the eyes of France,
and therefore among other reafons he oppofed
it, as neceffarily drawing on the invafion of
the electorate. However, the fupport of his
Majefty as elector was voted. France haftened
to poffefs herfelf of Hanover; fhe fucceeded:
a neutrality was figned. The troops of the
electorate and its allies were all but prifoners of
war, and the Duke of Brunfwick was treated
by France in terms only fit for a vaffal, and
native fubject of the crown of France. The
victory at Rofbach by the King of Pruffia at
length turned the tide of fuccefs againft
France. From the moment in which the
electoral troops and allies took up arms in the
name of Great Britain, to avoid being made
prifoners of war, and for infringements of the
capitulation, on the part of France, the whole
war in Germany became fatal to the French
nation; about 100,000 of its beft troops are
faid to have perifhed by famine, fword, and

fick-

ficknefs in one campaign. France had miftaken the magnanimity of the late King, as
the houfe of Auftria had miftaken his principle of nice adherence to public faith. Neither the war in Germany, nor the fufferings
of his electoral fubjects, prevented his Majefty
from pufhing the war in the Eaft Indies and
America, attacking the French coafts, and
deftroying their commerce. The fupport
of the war in Germany, however objection-
able had been the firft engaging in it,
as it could not be quitted with honour now,
and as circumftances were changed, was
adopted as a fecondary and fubordinate meafure with a view of diverting the whole force
and attention of France from the principal
object between her and Great Britain; which
was the poffeffion of that part of America
which is capable of fupplying us with fhip tim-
ber, feamen, naval ftores, and of being a conftant fource of induftry, population, and confequently of the moft extenfive national power.
France felt her miftake, fhe began to treat and
would

would willingly have withdrawn her troops from Hanover, as a firft preliminary; thereby fhowing that fhe thought the war there more ruinous to herfelf than burthenfome to England. France prevaricated; the preliminaries were broke off; and the fame efforts were exerted on the part of the Britifh nation as before.

The crifis is at length arrived, my Lord; and though another nation fince has entered weakly into the views of France, all that is our own in the American world which was our object of the war, and an immenfe acceffion of other poffeffions, more than is fufficient to indemnify us. The great queftion then is, how we fhall fit down?

· We are not mad enough to hope the total conqueft of our rival nations, becaufe that is impoffible, and not for our interefts; and I think the inference to be drawn from the facts ftated is very plain, that the fyftem of America

and

and the oriental world ought not *intirely* and
folely to preponderate in the fcale of negotiation
againſt all the relations this country ſtands in
neceſſarily, as a part of Europe. As private
men of great wealth and power derive ſtill
greater influence from equity, humanity, and
moderation, ſo a nation which may be termed
dominant with reſpect to the reſt of Europe
ſhould proceed in all its negotiations upon the
fame honeſt principles, and leave the arts of
leſs ſincerity and leſs equity and moderation
to inferior and little powers, to whom the
fineſſe of negotiation may be ſometimes neceſ-
fary for preſervation, as the only ballance
againſt a ſuperior force.

The celebrated Cardinal d'Oſſat, Em-
baſſador of Henry IV. of France at the
court of Rome, the ſchool of refined negotiation, where he ſucceeded in a moſt intri-
cate and ſtubborn buſineſs, uſed to ſay that
there was but one good method of nego-
tiating; an open hand and an open heart;
and

and that to gain confidence was to gain every thing.

Congreſſes oftener deſtroy confidence than haſten pacifications where many powers are concerned. There are many precedents of treaties and diſquiſitions upon public law, but the noble plainneſs of our admirals and military commanders in their capitulations granted to the enemy during their late expeditions is worth all the parade of Embaſſadors at a congreſs: and notwithſtanding the practice of negotiators and ſtateſmen in general, who attach themſelves to the pedantry of old forms, there ſeems to be no reaſon why treaties of the moſt comprehenſive kind may not be carried on with as much ſimplicity and pre-ciſion in ſtile, form, and matter, as the capi-tulation of a garriſon. This method of nego-tiating, natural enough to a nation which ne-gotiates with victorious arms in its hands, and which ought to command its allies, and not to be commanded by them, would indeed be

for

for the public fervice, but it might poffibly
leffen the importance of men interefted in
ceremonies and a train of fineffe and details,
calculated to fhew their talents, to amufe and
dazzle the people, but which create delay,
and, what is worfe, a diftruft of fincerity
between the powers who are principals in the
negotiation.

My Lord, I take it to be the intereft of
England to proceed at this crifis with the
utmoft fincerity; nothing can anfwer happier
purpofes than the laying afide every term of
infult to her enemies in defpair, and every
immoderate demand which may one day or
other excite the fame jealoufy and confederacy
among the reft of the powers of Europe againft
herfelf as the infolent behaviour of France
in her higheft point of profperity occafioned
once to her ambitious monarch. The plan
of pacification on the part of Great Britain
muft naturally be entered upon with a retrofpect to the caufe of the war, and with the
con-

confideration of the value of the poffeffions
conquered from the enemy now in her hands,
as the two great and leading principles. If
we can procure a fufficient indemnification
for thofe our unhappy allies, who have been
like the *Socii* and *Latini* in the Roman military eftablifhment and who formed by much
the greateft part of the Roman army, it will
be but juftice to thofe who have fought our
battles, and feen their own country reduced
for our fakes to defolation by all the horrors
of a long and revengeful war: if we can
fecure our colonies from any future dangers ;
if we can retain a fufficient fource of future
naval armaments for ourfelves without being
obliged to mean compliances with northern
nations in Europe, our inferiors, for fupplies
in times of difficulty; if we can alfo, over and
above, retain as much as we can conveniently
garrifon, without the places ceded to us proving
the grave of our feamen and foldiers ; if we can
obtain ample damages for our expences, and fit
down with an increafe of trade greatly fuperior

to that which we poffeffed at the outfet of the war, and fuch as may tend to add to our population and real ftrength by encouraging induftry, not by adding to our vices, luxury, and profufion; if thefe great ends can be accomplifhed by any plan of pacification fuppofed to be now under the confideration of thofe great perfons who have the honour to advife his Majefty, then, my Lord, I hope you and every candid and good man will hold them juftified, by carrying fuch a pacification boldly into execution: nay more, will think that it is their duty to feize an opportunity of compleating that which one fatal accident in the mutability of human things may prevent from ever returning; that the courage of any fervant of the King and public would be highly laudable in fuch a cafe; that a clamour would be ungrateful, and a difcontented oppofition almoft difloyalty.

Thus, my Lord, I have defcended into a plain narrative of a few facts and principles which

which have operated and will operate probably, whether there fhall be a continuance of the war, or a pacification fhall take place ; and whether one man or another is now or fhall be hereafter underftood to be the immediate director of public counfels. In fuch a light I hope this detail will have great utility, and I thought it proper to drop all affectation of a declamatory ftile in a feries of paft facts, which are the grounds of future expectation, and in which plain words are more eligible than a prodigality of that enriched language which often ferves only to cover truth with flowers, and to keep the principal fubject out of view.

Every attempt to be plain in a differtation of this kind will hardly, my Lord, be difapproved of by you, who know fo well how much a fimplicity of thinking has recommended the authors I have frequently quoted. They were not, like moft of our political writers, of the dregs and manners of the

people,

people, but they were men of the higheſt charaƈters in the ſtate, or converſant with thoſe who were ſo. We live in an age when our proſe, our poetry, our very politics, are ſet upon ſtilts and ſhewn off to the crowd. A pomp of words, a myſterious obſcurity, an air of paradox and refinement, but, what is worſt of all, a virulence of perſonality of the loweſt kind, infeƈt our writings and debates *pro aris et focis*, and inſure too often the ap-plauſe, and admiration of the multitude. But in treating every ſubjeƈt of public importance, a little plain reaſoning and a great deal of ho-neſty would be much more uſeful to the cauſe of truth and the intereſts of our country, than all our affeƈtation of eloquence; whether it flows turbid like the Saone or the Rhone in their conflux, or like the Thames, the Rhine and the Danube, in all the power and ma-jeſty of exuberance.

I am afraid my imagination too has carried me beyond bounds: I am concerned to find that

that a few undifciplined thoughts have thus run out into a long differtation: in which I have faid many things to yourfelf, many *ad homines*, and *ad populum*, but I hope more *ad veritatem*. However, the importance of the fubject at this juncture will apologize for endeavouring to take as comprehenfive a view as poffible of the public interefts. It is befides fome confolation to me, that it is in every reader's power to make the whole of thefe confiderations as fhort as he pleafes; and I do affure him, like Balzac, that if I had had more time I would have made them a great deal fhorter; as well as have endeavoured to avoid thofe marks of hafte and even of rapidity, which I am too fenfible and afhamed that they now carry with them. I fhall conclude therefore, my Lord, in recommending once more, and too often, I dare fay you think, it cannot be recommended, unanimity to my countrymen, whatever fyftem of public conduct they fhall at laft adhere to; and above all to follow that folid and ufeful maxim for pre-

ferving

serving the interefts of all public focieties whatfoever, " that the minorities after the firft
" ftruggle fhould yield to and unite with ma-
" jorities ;" fo that there may be one whole
collected force of government moving as one
man, and actuated by one fpirit for the general good : that we may think of combating
nothing but falfe opinions recently adopted,
or old prejudices grown up with us, leaving
it to men of weak minds and ftrong paffions
to attack nominal diftinctions with as much
vehemence as the knight of la Mancha en-
countered windmills, becaufe he thought them
giants; but above all endeavouring with our
utmoft efforts, that public confiderations fhould
prevail over private interefts at this great crifis,
with every order of men amongft us, fo far as
human nature will permit us to indulge the
hope.

Your rank, my Lord, your character, and
influence, the magnanimity of his Majefty, the
firmnefs, and the integrity of his fervants will
greatly

greatly contribute to this falutary end. In the mean time, unattached to any fet of men or meafures, excepting the regard I have the honour to profefs for your perfonal happinefs, reputation and intereft, and my zeal to be in a more particular manner the *Advocate of his Majefty*, whofe good intentions deferve the moft grateful return from his people, I fhall content myfelf with imitating, as well as I can,

The good Erafmus in an honeft mean,

preaching concord, and praying for the public peace, as warmly and as fruitlefsly perhaps as he did for the peace of the church, in times of general diffenfion; when a number of parties divided and fubdivided, paffing to the very utmoft extremities, the common intereft and happinefs of all men which laid in the center were torn in pieces. I dread that the fame kind of fcene is again approaching, when men tired out with their own happinefs and fuccefs will in the heart of the ftate heap faction upon faction, and that our greateft ene-

mies

mies will then be able to pronounce, and even to fee fulfilled againft this nation the curfe denounced by the Roman againft the enemies of Rome.

Maneat quæfo, duretque gentibus, fi non amor noftri, at certè odium fui ; quando urgentibus imperii fatis, nihil jam præftare fortuna majus poteft quam hoftium difcordiam.

I am, my Lord, &c.

www.ingramcontent.com/pod-product-compliance
Lightning Source LLC
Chambersburg PA
CBHW032103010726
47493CB00008B/2511